Hoa Pham is a psychologist, author and playwright. She has written seven previous books. Her novella *Wave*, published by Spinifex Press in 2015, has been optioned as a film, and rights for a translation have been sold to Vietnam. Hoa won the Best Young Writer Award from the Sydney Morning Herald for her novel *Vixen*. *The Other Shore* won the Viva La Novella Prize. Her play *Silence* was on the VCE drama list in 2010. Hoa is also the founder of *Peril* magazine, an Asian-Australian online arts and culture magazine.

Hoa has received funding support from the Australia Council of the Arts and has been on an Asialink residency in Vietnam, and fellowships at the Tyrone Guthrie Centre and the Goethe Institute Berlin. She has a doctorate in creative arts and also holds master degrees in both creative writing and psychology. She lives in Melbourne.

OTHER BOOKS BY HOA PHAM

Wave (2015)

The Other Shore (2014)

Silence (2010)

Vixen (2000)

Quicksilver (1999)

49 Ghosts (1998)

No-one Like Me (1998)

LADY OF THE REALM

HOA PHAM

Published in Australia by Spinifex Press, 2017

Spinifex Press Pty Ltd
PO Box 105
Mission Beach Qld 4852

www.spinifexpress.com.au
women@spinifexpress.com.au

Editor: Pauline Hopkins
Cover design: Deb Snibson
Typesetting: Helen Christie
Typeset in Times New Roman
Printed by McPherson's Printing Group

National Library of Australia Cataloguing-in-Publication data:
Pham, Hoa, 1972– author.
Lady of the realm / Hoa Pham.

9781925581133 (paperback)
9781925581157 (ebook)
9781925581140 (ebook: pdf)
9781925581164 (ebook: epub)

Vietnam—Social life and customs—Fiction.
Vietnam—Fiction.

  This project has been assisted by the Australian Government through the Australia Council, its arts funding and advisory body.

For Alister Air, my good heart,
and to the memory of Prajna Monastery, Vietnam
and Thích Nhất Hạnh
where I finally came home.

HISTORICAL NOTE

I have loosely based this novella on the following moments in history: the Vietnam/American War 1961–1975, and the exile of Thích Nhất Hạnh from Vietnam in 1966 (approximately 19 monks and nuns self-immolated during this period); the period of đổi mới in the 1980s in Vietnam to the opening up of Vietnam in the 1990s to 2000s to foreigners; and the destruction of Prajna Monastery by the Vietnamese government in 2009.

What is called the Vietnam War in the West is known in Vietnam as the American War. I use the latter term to reflect the viewpoint of the protagonists.

The Việt Minh was a communist political and paramilitary organisation originating in Northern Vietnam working to overthrow foreign influences in the country. Viet Cong was the term used by the US military for the forces they were fighting. There is some contention about the two terms and their usage. For my fictional purposes the Việt Minh describes the force in the North pre-1965 and the Viet Cong in the American War. The National Liberation Front is another term also used for the Viet Cong.

Hồ Chí Minh City is the official name for the city previously known as Saigon.

PROLOGUE

Looking back over the years, it seems that time stretches and contracts, depending on my experience of each moment. Some moments are etched in my memory, like the sunlight patterning the water in the river, ethereal moments captured only by my mind. Other longer stretches of time are a blur, marked only by rituals and meditative pauses that remind me that I am still alive. More poignant are the memories of what I have lost, assuaged only after years of suffering by the wisdom and compassion I have gained.

Quan Âm listens to the sufferings of the world, as does the Lady of the Realm.

The past is entwined with the present, as is the future. Being mindful of each moment can make peace possible. I've only experienced peace for a few years, but having this experience makes me hopeful that times of peace can come again.

Unfortunately it will be too late for the dead.

HIẾU,
LOVE OF FAMILY
SOUTH VIETNAM, 1962

The story began long ago ... it is old.
Older than my body, my mother's, my grandmother's ...
For years we have been passing it on.
So our daughters and granddaughters
may continue to pass it on.

TRINH MINH-HÀ
Women, Native Other

Once I was young and carefree of the world. Those times seem idyllic to me, but only in recollection.

The Lady first called to me in a dream. I was pleasantly exhausted from another day of fishing with my family, the salt tang on my lips, caking my hair, covering my skin. I was wedged comfortably between my mother and my sister and fell into heavy sleep.

My dream was underwater. I could breathe and I walked on the ocean floor surrounded by brittle corals and bones. When I looked closer I saw rib cages and human skulls among the debris. Fish brushed past me, indifferent to my presence. Then I saw human bodies floating by, bloated on the ocean surface. Fishermen from my village, their blood trailing in the water.

Shocked awake, I sat up. I clutched at my mother's heavy body wanting her to reassure me. But she was sound asleep. In the darkness my eyes teared up at the vision of the dead people. What was the goddess trying to tell me?

I lay back down again and was sucked back into sleep.

In the morning I went to the đình, the village square, where a wooden effigy of the Lady of the Realm was kept in the centre hall. Bowing to Bà, my grandmother, who tended the shrine, I clutched a bunch of purple wildflowers for the Lady, and a rice cake from my breakfast. Bà opened up the hall for me and bade me enter.

I bowed to the wooden figurine shrouded in the shade of the morning sun. She wore a bright pink cloth veil made by my grandmother, and her serene face bore a half-smile. The hall always had a hush about it due to the meditating and worship for the Lady and I walked slowly on the hallowed ground.

7

Bà stood behind me as I offered my flowers to the goddess. As I recounted my dream my fingers began to tremble and I wished to cry again.

"Child that is a dire dream," Bà told me. She enveloped me in her arms and I received the comfort I rarely received from my busy mother.

"It's a message from the goddess."

"But who would kill our people like that?" I asked innocently.

"Invaders from the North. The Việt Minh want to control all of Vietnam," Bà told me.

"What do we do?"

"I will tell our village head. We should post watchmen to look out while we are fishing and plan our hiding places. And we shall pray to the Lady of the Realm and thank her for her warning."

I nodded, reassured. The village head, Bác, was grandmother's nephew and would do what she said. I bowed again before the Lady, and prayed to her that my dream would not come to pass.

But my stomach still cramped with misery from my dream and my tears still threatened when I went out to help gut the fish from the morning catch.

"What's wrong with you?" snapped my sister.

"I had a nightmare," I mumbled, knowing better than to ask for sympathy.

"Hhhmph!" she dismissed turning her attention back to Học, the fisherman she had been flirting with.

I turned back to the messy fish guts on my hands and wanted to vomit. Swallowing bile I willed myself not to be sick, though all I wanted to do was to curl up in bed.

That afternoon was the day of my first bleeding. I first thought I had wet myself during our afternoon nap-time. I bled through my pants and snuck out to the river to wash them in shame. I was so miserable I did not notice Bà until she put a comforting hand on my shoulder.

"You are now a woman Liên," Bà told me proudly and patted me on the arm.

At that moment, it was the last thing I would have wished on anybody.

That afternoon I met up with Tài, my closest friend. He was standing in the river opening up the fish traps in the fast-running current.

"What's wrong Liên?" he asked, clambering up to me, after spotting my miserable hunched-up form by the riverbank.

I reddened under his caring gaze.

"I'm bleeding," I whispered embarrassed under my breath. "Like a woman," I added as he drew a shocked breath.

He put his arm companionably around me as if nothing had changed. He flicked his fingers showering me with little droplets of water and I smiled.

"You're still Liên," he said as if to reassure me. For the first time I looked at him side on and saw his profile anew. Just the other month his voice had broken, and I had teased him and his voice see-sawing like an opera singer. Now his chin was more manly and his voice settled deep. Then, as if aware of my gaze, he looked away.

"I had a dream from the Lady," I told him shyly. "The Việt Minh came and destroyed our village. They destroyed the statue of the Lady." Tears started in my eyes.

"Why would they come here? We have no gold. We're just fishermen."

I smiled tentatively wanting to believe him.

"So that is why they want me in the trees instead of on the river. I thought it was Bà's will no more. Are you going to be the mouthpiece of the Lady after Bà?"

I nodded.

He grinned at me and ruffled my hair.

"I always knew you were special, Liên," he said and leapt up to jump back into the river to fix the fish traps. His easy acceptance warmed me as much as the sun did that day.

The next morning we were woken up by a shout from Tài. A group of refugees were coming to the village! I ran with the others to the village đình to hear their news.

They were bloody and wounded, a couple of men, four women and just one child.

"The Việt Minh destroyed everything," their leader told us. He had only narrowly escaped with his life by pretending to be dead.

Carrying my breakfast offering in my hands for the Lady, I was shocked by the families straggled and bloody before us. The little boy stared at the breakfast cake in my hand.

Impulsively, I gave it to him.

The Lady would not mind, I thought. She looks after everyone and would not want him to go hungry.

The head of the village, Bác, stared at me.

"Liên," he indicated that I should step forward.

"Is this what you dreamed?"

Confronted by the stark reality of the survivors, I could only nod.

"Liên has been touched by the Lady of the Realm. She foresaw that this would happen."

I felt the attention of my village turn onto me and I wilted under their scrutiny.

"She is a virgin," whispered Học to one of the others. "That is why she has been touched by the goddess."

I felt my sister's anger and jealousy next to me, like a slow heat.

"What did you dream last night?" the head demanded.

I shook my head miserably. I did not want my dreams to come true.

"I dreamt of bones," I whispered softly.

"She dreams of bodies under the sea." Thankfully Bà stepped in for me. Her tortoiseshell hairpin glinted in the sun as she spoke.

Muttering arose like the whispering of waves amongst the village.

"We have to take heed of this warning," Bác said.

The refugees did not want to stay long. The village head generously gave them a fishing boat so they could sail out into the ocean and make landfall elsewhere. They warned us that the Việt Minh were close and we should abandon the village and run.

But Bác refused.

"We will know when they come. This is the land that we were born in. We will not abandon it so easily. The Lady will warn us when we should flee."

He looked to me and I wished I deserved the faith that he placed in my dreams.

Tai stood to one side, his arms crossed, frowning. There was none of his cocksure ease now. When the village meeting dissolved, he came to my side.

"Liên, I did not know that you dreamed true."

I looked away from him. Other people were staring at me, then at the refugees, as if I myself had turned into the Lady.

"I didn't know either," I admitted.

Tài looked at me a moment longer then touched my cheek with a finger. "I'd better go back on watch," he said, and ran back to the trees with his easy lope.

I brushed my cheek with a wondering hand as Bà came up beside me protectively.

"Liên needs to rest," she told the curious villagers who used to scold me and regard me as no more than another of the village cats.

I felt their eyes upon me as I walked slowly back to our dwelling alone.

That night the refugees stayed in the village đình, sleeping under the watchful eye of the Lady of the Realm. My father stayed up late in the night talking to them, trying to discover what the Northerners were wanting. My mother, sister and I huddled in our house, waiting for his return.

"We must pray to the Lady that they do not come here," mother said. She brushed my hair gently, for the first time in months. Her tenderness touched me. Usually mother was too exhausted and had no time. But tonight she tended both my sister and me. When I haltingly told her about my period, she nodded and showed me how to knot the rags around my waist better to staunch the bleeding.

Father came home frowning. He seemed to have aged since talking to the refugees.

"Tell us more about your dream," he rapped out to me impatiently.

"I told Bác everything," I said miserably. I did not want my dreams to come true, and I was getting cramps from my period.

"You must tell us if you dream again," Father told me. He turned to Mother and they whispered in the dark as if we could not understand. I lay next to my sister, wide awake, wondering what it was they hid from us. I feared to dream again. What would happen if all my dreams came true? I remembered the bloated face of Học floating by in the ocean.

I had not seen my own family. What did that mean?

"Lady …" I whispered in the darkness. Moving my lips silently I formed my own prayers to her while my parents finally fell silent and asleep.

The next morning when I woke, my family were already clustered around me.

"Did you dream?" my sister pounced in first. I shook my head.

"You're nothing special," my sister jibed at me when mother's back was turned.

Mother gave me a cup of tea and my favourite rice cake with an egg yolk in the middle.

When I came out to do my morning duties and visit the Lady of the Realm, half the village was clustered around the đình. The refugees were sitting in the sun, eating breakfast. Their eyes were wide open and they were exhausted as if they had not slept at all. Bác came over to me at once and bowed his head as if I was my grandmother.

"Did you dream?" he asked.

"No I did not," I replied helplessly.

He took me by the elbow and escorted me to the centre of the hall to the Lady of the Realm. Bà had shrouded her in white cloth. The offerings laid out for her were like a banquet – fish wrapped in banana leaves, fruit, flowers and sweets.

Bà was waiting there, clipping her tortoiseshell hairpin into her bun. I was glad when Bác left me alone with her.

"Did you dream, child?" Bà asked, and from her, the query was kind and gentle, not the interrogation of my family and my village. She was concerned about me not just the contents of my dream.

I shook my head wanting to cry. I could feel the eyes of the other villagers and the refugees on me, as if I were the Lady of the Realm. I could not shake off the empty hugeness of the refugees' eyes. They clutched at me as if for luck, touching me like they would touch her statue.

"How is your bleeding?" Bà whispered to me as I stood up from bowing to the Lady of the Realm.

"It hurts."

"Come with me and I'll brew some herbal medicine for you."

I followed my grandmother to our now empty house. She sat me down and sorted through some medicinal herbs to boil.

"Will the Lady of the Realm protect us?" I asked her.

"She is protecting us by sending warnings to you, little Liên." Bà said.

"Why me?" I tried not to whimper.

Bà turned from putting the herbs on to boil and touched my head lightly.

"The Lady speaks most to those who listen for her," she said cryptically and I frowned.

I knew that I was Bà's favourite and when she died, I was to succeed her as keeper of the Lady. My sister wanted a husband and my parents were too busy fishing.

"Why didn't she warn the other village?" I asked.

Bà sighed and sat down next to me.

"Perhaps she did and no one heard her." Bà began plaiting some long grasses together with flowers to make a garland for the Lady.

"I will hear her," I declared. I did not want the village to be pillaged and my family killed.

"The whole village has heard her now," Bà said. "We have to protect ourselves."

During the days that followed the village made more offerings to the Lady of the Realm. I was included in the worship. They began to offer me the choicest portions of our meals, and would not take a refusal for an answer. Gifts began appearing at our house. Mother would fawn over the presents and take them, and my sister's presence was like a thundercloud. Even Học, my older sister's fancy, started paying attention to me. First he asked me about my dreams. I told him what I told all the villagers. I did not want to tell him about how his corpse's shocked open eyes had transfixed me in the dream. Then one day he brought me some purple flowers.

My sister saw the flowers and stamped on them, grinding them into the ground.

"You shouldn't have done that," I told her through my tears. "They were for the Lady of the Realm."

My sister snorted at my naïveté. "I'm not too old for Học. You are too young," she snarled at me before storming out, refusing to sleep next to me and my foreboding dreams.

Only one person did not treat me any differently after Bà recounted my dream to the village elders. Tài. He still splashed water on me when I went by the river and teased me good-naturedly.

I visited him every day climbing up his favourite trees where he would perch and look out over the hills. From up there the village was small, surrounded by the square bamboo fence that marked out our village from the fields around.

We would sit close together, shoulders touching, and we would make up stories together to pass the time. My favourites were the miracle stories of the Lady of the Realm where she would make herself known and save villages by her divine intervention.

Sometimes we would be so engrossed, we forgot about the threat of the Việt Minh invasion. But other days it was all we would talk about.

"If the Việt Minh come this way you have to run," Tài said to me one day. "Don't wait for anyone."

"But what about Bà?" I could not leave her in the village.

"Bà will protect the Lady of the Realm," he said. "And in return the Lady will protect her. You are a young girl. You will be in danger."

I stared at him quizzically. I saw my reflection in his eyes. I was becoming a woman, and I wasn't a young girl anymore, I thought rebelliously. Then I realised what he meant.

"What would we do if the Việt Minh come here and defile the Lady?" I asked. The refugees from other villages had told us that they destroyed everything they saw.

Tai sighed for a moment looking out onto the horizon.

"The Lady will come to you in dreams, Liên. If our village is destroyed, maybe you should try and find her. Bring her back to save us."

Then he smiled at me and my heart lifted at his lightness.

That night I had a beautiful dream. I was breathing in and out at the base of a giant white marble Buddha in the trees. Young novices in brown played in a waterfall beneath me. The sun shone and instinctively I knew that we were in a time of peace. The Buddha smiled down on me and in the distance I could hear chanting of the Heart Sutra.

I woke up to a sense of peace that I have never felt in real life.

I shared my dream with Bà and Bà smiled.

"We can look forward to seeing the giant Buddha in the future. Once President Diem is gone, the Buddhists will be able to restore the spirits of the people."

"Does the Lady of the Realm mind me praying to Buddha?"

"No. She is in the guise of Quan Âm who hears the cries of the world with the Buddhists. The true spirits are not jealous of their followers' faiths."

So as well as my daily prayer to the Lady, I prayed to Quan Âm and the Buddha too.

But to no avail.

Later that day I asked Bà where I could find the Lady.

"The Lady is with you always, little Liên," Bà told me. She stroked my wrist with wrinkled fingers. She was the only one that ever told me I was beautiful.

"That's not what I mean. Just suppose they come here and destroy her. Then where would I find her?" I asked.

Bà patted the ground next to me and I sat down cross-legged in front of the wooden hall. Inside the hall incense was burning and the smoke tickled my nose.

"I won't desert you, Bà, or the Lady," I declared, putting my arms around her.

Bà smiled then tilted my chin with a wizened finger.

"Child, if the Việt Minh come, you must hide. I will hide as well and afterwards we will escape to the mountains. Don't come looking for me. I'm cleverer than any Northerner!"

I chuckled with her.

That afternoon I gave the best portion of my meal to the Lady of the Realm. Her statue was garlanded with leaves and daisies, and her smile was freshly painted.

"Protect us Lady," I prayed.

Unexpectedly the next morning, Father took a day off fishing.
I had not slept well, fearing my dreams, and my sister had to coax me awake by pinching me.

"We have to ensure that our ancestors look after us," Father muttered an explanation and even helped Mother cook up extra cakes for our ancestral graves.

We followed him, first Father and Mother, then me and my sister trailing behind, carrying the offerings. When we came to the village cemetery, Father found the mounds where Grandfather was buried and made a deep bow. Bà joined us with sticks of smoking incense and she murmured prayers for the ancestors.

"We cannot leave our ancestors' land," Father said to Mother, as if bringing up an old argument. "Who else will look after their memories?"

"We can't if we are dead!" Mother protested too loudly.

"No one is going to die. Little Liên will warn us," Father said proudly.

I gulped. My nightmares had been getting worse. I wanted to say that the warnings were to be acted on, and the Lady did not send them lightly. I wanted to say that Mother was right.

But I was still too scared of Father and too uncertain of myself. This I would regret for the rest of my life.

That night the dream came earlier. I felt the bones crunch under my feet and the metallic taste of blood in my mouth. When I woke, I spat out blood. I had bitten my tongue. It was still night. My stomach cramped and I could not sleep.

I went out to the village đình to visit the Lady. The night was cool from the sea breeze. Then I saw a flash of metal amongst the trees.

Immediately I froze. I turned around and walked slowly back towards where my family were sleeping. As soon as I was within the shadow of houses, I ran straight to my mother and shook her by the shoulder.

"They're here!" I whispered fiercely. She jolted awake and woke my sister with a prod.

"We must warn the others. Liên, prepare the boats."

We ran from our home on quiet feet. I headed towards the beach where our boats were resting upside down from the last catch. On the way, I thought of Tài and Bà. After I prepared the boats I would find them, I told myself.

The night was dark with only a fingernail sliver of the moon in the sky. Among our fishing boats, I struggled to turn them over one at a time, as quietly as possible.

Then the sound of the bell rang through our village. It rang urgently. Once, twice, thrice.

I had only overturned two boats as the first families came out onto the beach.

Men rushed to help me. Bà and my mother and sister were nowhere to be seen.

We scraped the first boat along the shore and it seemed like the very weight of the boat was holding us back from our escape. Sand grated on my feet as I pulled the prow into the ocean with the men. We had launched the first boat of women and children into the sea when the Northerners appeared on the beach. Our fisherman advanced on them with wooden staves and I despaired.

I helped with the second boat and shoved it into the sea.

Then a Việt Minh appeared out of nowhere. Someone screamed.

He grabbed me and I struggled. He tore at my pants and grabbed my groin.

Then he dropped me as his hands came away sticky with my monthly blood. I landed with a thud on the sand. He threw himself on top of me and I struggled as he forced his way inside me. Pain lanced through my insides and I screamed, beating him futilely with my hands.

Then he saw the fracas on the beach, shoved me aside and ran to join in.

Terrified I staggered to my feet, hearing the scrape of a boat being pulled into the sea. I pulled up my pants and stumbled over to help.

More desperate hands grabbed at me.

"Come with us, Liên," and I was lifted reluctantly into the boat as it ploughed into the sea. On the beach the men I knew from birth were being slaughtered.

I helped with the rowing and the launch of the sail. Our gazes were pinned to the shore. Our village was lit up in silhouette by fire.

Children cried as the women prayed and murmured the mantras to the Lady of the Realm.

But she did not come to save us.

We stayed out at sea until the sun rose. My throat ached with thirst and my eyes were swollen from crying. Smoke smudged the horizon as we searched the shoreline with weary eyes for signs of survivors.

"Has the Lady spoken to you?" one of the women asked me, grabbing my sleeve desperately.

I shook my head, biting my lip, not wanting to meet the hope in their eyes. I feared the worst as we beached the boats up from the village in a small cove. We could only hope to sneak back to our village to discover if the Việt Minh had stayed or not.

I resented the murmur of the women and children around me. I wanted Bà to hold me, and my family to be creeping back to the village, not these others.

I looked up into the trees to see if Tài was there.

He was not.

The forest was eerily quiet as if nothing had happened.

Then we tripped over the first body. It was Học, bullet wounds seeping from his back. He had been running away. Where was my sister? He should have been with my sister!

I clambered up a nearby tree to look down at the smouldering ruins of our village. The village đình was destroyed, a blackened stain on the land. I saw bodies scattered around the ruins of houses. But I was so far up I could not tell who they were.

There was no movement. I waited for a while but the only thing that moved was a stray chicken running across the ashes. Trembling, I returned to the ground. The remaining villagers' eyes were round, the devastated look of refugees.

I could not speak, only stammer out what I saw. "I think they have gone," I said, and they mutely accepted.

Carefully, we went back to the village. I scouted ahead with another child. The smell of smoke, ash and burning flesh filled our senses. I began coughing and couldn't stop.

More bodies. I turned them over, my stomach churning. None of them were Việt Minh. They were all the people I had grown up with, shot for no reason.

The Việt Minh had massacred the village.

I found the remains of Father at the đình. Hot tears streaked down my face as I searched for Bà. The Lady of the Realm's statue was reduced to a stump. Ashes were hot under my feet as I circled the remains of the village in ever widening circles.

As if from a large distance, I could hear the others wailing and crying.

My mother and sister were nowhere to be found. Then I found Bà's hairpin made of tortoiseshell in what was once our house. The bodies in our house were burnt beyond recognition. One of them could have been Tài trying to find me.

I wanted to vomit at the smell.

Clutching the hairpin, I retreated out of the village and went back to the beach where the fishing boats were. The remaining boats had been set alight and destroyed.

I collapsed on the sand, weeping.

When I came to, the other villagers had clustered around me sitting dazed on the sand. They were looking at me expectantly as if I could say something, do something that would save them all.

"The Lady has deserted us," I said bitterly. She had not protected Bà, and Bà had worshipped her all her life.

The others started muttering amongst themselves.

"Where can we go now?" one child cried forlornly, echoing what we were all thinking.

"South," a woman said. "What do you think, Liên?"

I stared back at her. They were expecting me to lead them.

I nodded helplessly. Even if I was gifted with prescience from the Lady, what use was it? The Việt Minh still came. Despite our precautions, the village was dead.

From the others, I learnt that none of the dead were women or children. The Việt Minh had taken them away. They began to discuss whether they could follow and rescue them. A group of women and children, we would be captured ourselves, I thought.

"We need an army to get them back," I said.

Where would we find an army?

"South," I replied. The larger Vietnamese towns would take us in. Some of them had military garrisons.

We gathered together without speaking. We were too frightened to stay around the village to bury the dead, just in case the Việt Minh came back. I bowed and prayed to the centre of the village for the newly deads' forgiveness. Behind me, the others followed suit.

I bundled up my hair and stuck my short bun through with my grandmother's tortoiseshell hairpin. Then I led the refugees back into the forest to head to Saigon.

UPEKSHA,
LOVE THAT GOES BEYOND
ALL BOUNDARIES

SAIGON, 1964

The heart of the prajnaparamita.

*The Boddhisattava Avalokita while moving in the
deep course of the Perfect Wisdom shed light on the
five aggregates and found them all equally empty.
After this penetration he overcame all pain ...*

THE HEART SUTRA

My dreams were lanced by fire and carnage. I feared sleeping but was so exhausted from running every day that I crashed regardless. Then I dreamt again of a waterfall and the white Buddha.

It was the only thing that gave me hope.

Guided by this dream I sought refuge at the largest Buddhist monastery in Saigon. Surrounded by traffic, its courtyard was an oasis of calm amongst the hustle of the city. When I stepped into the meditation hall and heard the murmur of monks and their mantras, I was reminded of peace again.

Na-mo A-vo-li-ke-te-ra. Na-mo A-vo-li-ke-te-ra.

I bowed to the white and gold porcelain statue of Quan Âm overlooking the shrine to the departed dead. Her smile was tranquil, and just looking at the curve of her cheeks made my soul settle inside once more. The Buddha inside the main meditation hall was gold, not the white of my dream. But I knew not to ignore my dream's significance.

I had heard good things about this monastery, their most prominent monk Thích Nhất Hạnh` who had founded the School of Youth and Social Service. They were looking for volunteers to practice engaged Buddhism, to help out those suffering because of the American War. Both women and men joined the SYSS.

My fellow villagers took to the pho kitchen and rested in the shadow of the giant gold Buddha that overlooked the meditation hall.

I wondered whether I would be able to pray for the Lady on this holy ground. I was angry at what had befallen us and wanted to do something, anything. Maybe the SYSS was one way to assuage the damage that the Việt Minh had done. Maybe working for the temple will help peace. In my dream I was in a monastic's robes. Perhaps I can make my dream come true.

So I signed up to volunteer. They assigned me a mentor, a young nun with merry bright eyes whose happiness and enthusiasm infused me with good heart. I was to be her assistant.

Hương was beautiful and her smile was full of light. I tried to return her smile but I could not; my heart was too heavy from what I had seen. Her spontaneity and warmth lifted me out of my bitterness, and I suddenly longed to be like her, and be able to be open of heart again.

The days of mindfulness in the temple were a source of joy to me. Each action in the monastery was done with mindfulness with my brothers and sisters.

Washing the dishes. Dipping our hands into the soapy water and feeling the rinse of each plate. Sweeping the floor, concentrating on each sweep to and fro. Hearing the birds in the courtyard and the murmur of voices in a new fresh way.

We would meditate together and my practice picked up and deepened, surrounded by the concentration of all those around me. My consciousness would relax and extend beyond my body in the stillness of the *sangha*, the community. When I opened my eyes, my gaze would rest on the painting of the Buddha on the scrolls in the hall. He was serene, his half smile reflecting the calm within.

Present moment, wonderful moment. I am fresh as a flower.

I am as still as a mountain.

I am like water reflecting.

I went to the main meditation hall where the Buddha was gold not white. I prayed for the time to come, I now knew better than to ignore my dreams. I was waiting for my prescience to come true. I would not be killed by war and Vietnam could achieve peace.

Hương and I stepped onto our rusty old bicycles to ride out into the country where our help was most needed. As we rode over dirt tracks criss-crossed and rough from many people travelling, I saw the ravines of destruction across the green rice paddy fields that once were harvested in season. They were blackened with fires. A small shrine had been blasted apart and shrapnel lay everywhere. It was hard to winkle people out of hiding. It was not until Hương had stopped in a clearing and rung a bell three times that their curiosity got the better of them, so they emerged from the ruins of their villages.

I witnessed despair and horror pulling me back in bitterness. Hương never faltered, except the furrow of her brow became deeper. Now when she smiled occasionally at me, it was wan and sick. She taught me how to wash wounds and bandage the hurts and burns of the people. I could only nod in empathy at the stories people told, of women raped, and men and children slaughtered. This was familiar to me, too familiar.

War was always the same. Men causing carnage while the victims died with no time for proper burial or grieving.

Then Hương stopped for a rest. She seated herself down on a dry patch of earth and bid me do the same. We breathed in and meditated together.

When I closed my eyes and let go of the horrible things I had seen, at the sound of her bell I found myself returning me to that island of calm I had cultivated while meditating at the temple in Saigon.

31

Present moment, wonderful moment.

It was her intense practice and the days of mindfulness that kept her fresh and rejuvenated, I realised. When I opened my eyes and met her gaze, finally I was able to smile again.

The work with the wounded took its toll on us both. Sometimes Hương would have tears in her eyes when she saw how much the little children were maimed in the war. I too broke down and we comforted each other, hugging one another. The simple human touch made me feel closer to her.

She would sing, simple songs inspired by Thầy as we called Thích Nhất Hạnh, Vietnamese for teacher.

I have arrived, I am home.

In the here and in the now.

I am solid, I am free.

Her voice was like a lark's and I soon learned I could join her with my own voice, strengthened by the healing of the practice.

Thầy's teachings talked about helping others, in engaged Buddhism and applying the Heart Sutra in a renewed way. He introduced me to the concept of interbeing — that everything is inter-connected and inter-are.

Form is emptiness, emptiness is form and we are all connected together. Thus we have to treat others and ourselves with compassion.

Hương and I talked about the Heart Sutra and it was then that I felt as close to her as I did to Bà. I had found a mentor steeped in the practice, open and generous, and willing to share her wisdom. Hương loved the simplicity of Thầy's teachings.

We are the continuation of our ancestors and we will open our hearts with compassion to others to become more human.

Thầy said that the Buddha was a man and a human being. He did not worship the Buddha as God. Thầy's teachings were radical and new. He was influenced greatly by his time in France and America and knew how to make Buddhism easy for the lay people.

I dreamt of the ivory Buddha in the trees again. When I awoke next to Hương, I felt hope for the first time since leaving our village. Maybe my gift had a benefit after all.

I found myself opening up to Hương during our discussions of the dharma. We would sit in the courtyard where questions had begun to fester in my mind. A lark sang amongst the bare branches of the trees and the gentle murmur of the mantras of the monks made me brave enough to speak my mind.

"I am still angry at the Việt Minh and I do not trust them."

She gently touched my hand and smiled sadly. "The Việt Minh have many on their side. But you need to take care of your anger. They have been ordered to kill the ones we see here. But if we were brought up to kill, we too would be like them and wish to conquer all."

I was silent for a while, and looked out into the busy courtyard from the bench we were sitting on. People were lining up for breakfast pho amongst the topiary of hedge animals tended by the nuns and monks.

"I could kill if I had a gun and someone wanted to kill me," I said recklessly.

Hương looked sideways at me.

"Killing is never sanctioned by the Buddha. The seeds of violence in you have been watered very much. Watered in all of us, in fact. Mind your fear and your anger. Your practice is very deep, Liên. Draw on it like you would draw water from a well. I understand your suffering, but killing only makes us suffer more."

I bit my tongue then and sighed. Focusing inwards I took another breath before I spoke again.

"I want the war to stop," I explained. "I don't want any more killing."

"Thầy is in America asking them to stop the war," Hương reminded me. "We can send energy to him in our prayers."

This seemed like naive advice to me, so I held my tongue then. But she knew more than I did, I soon learned and had no fear.

I aspired to be like Hương, and have a mind free from suffering. She somehow was able to approach even the worst war wounds with equanimity by breathing in and out.

One day as we sat drinking water out in the country, I found myself opening up to her like a flower. I looked at her peaceful face, her dark eyes deep like lacquer and the years of mindfulness that radiated from her like the calm ripples from a pond.

"Today I remember my mother," Hương said suddenly.

With the sensitivity I had acquired over spending days and weeks with her, I heard her personal sorrow and a story to be told.

"She did not want me to abandon my family and join the SYSS. But I was the fourth daughter and useless to everyone at home …"

I opened my mouth to reject such a sentiment but her gaze was far away.

"She screamed at me that Thích Nhất Hạnh is a poet. A dreamer. That he did not know anything and how could he do anything about the war. But I had to work and hope. It is better to do that than to wait to be slaughtered by the Americans or the National Liberation Front."

Then Hương bowed her head in silence. In the rice paddies, crows called across the fields in the distance.

"My parents died last year. I was not there so I did not die." Her eyes glistened then the tears receded.

I touched her hand gently and she smiled, a different smile of grief.

I hugged her in the way I had seen the other nuns hug each other for comfort like children. She thanked me gently. Then she smiled again, a smile only for me and I felt my spirits lift.

Hương had suffered the way I had suffered, losing her family to the wars. Here was someone who had suffered yet still had enough compassion to heal others. She was a *bodhisattva* in her plain robe and muddy feet.

"Thank you for being here with me and sharing." She put her hands together and bowed to me.

"A lotus to you, sister," I said formally and bowed back. I wanted to share something with her, to make our intimacy two-way. So I found myself telling her of the dreams I had, of the carnage and destruction, and then the peace I had with the Buddha.

She was lost in thought as I spoke and I soon came to a shuddering halt with my words.

"Liên …" she reached out and touched my hand. "Do you see peace in your dreams?"

"Yes. I do. I am sitting on a grey rock in lotus position looking out over a waterfall. There is peace within me and outside of me."

She smiled suddenly and radiantly and I could not help but share that smile.

"It is because of that dream that I can keep living." I told her the honest bare truth of my existence. "One day there will be peace in Vietnam. But not before more war occurs."

Hương sobered up again and gazed at the plump brown sparrows gathered around our feet. Back at the temple we would catch them with grain and release them for luck for the lay people.

"That gives me hope," she said and we shared the rest of the day in noble silence.

One morning Hương surprised me with a new request.

"I have a letter to Thầy. Could you keep it for me today?"

Overwhelmed by her confidence in me I nodded and tucked the letter away in my pouch. I accompanied her as I did every day with first aid materials into the streets. Last night the bombers had been quiet, which filled me with dread. Usually the silence preceded a larger barrage that killed and injured more people.

Hương radiated calm that day, a deeper sense that radiated out to me. I could not worry for long as she walked mindfully with each step, feeling the miracle that we were still alive.

Children seeing our robes ventured out into the street, dodging the rubble and missile shells. Soon the word had spread and the injured and maimed came to us.

We tended to them, and my hands soon became sticky with blood, gore and pus. Each story I heard made me despair further. One village was occupied by the Việt Minh at night and in the daytime the Army of the Republic of Vietnam, the ARVN, would hold the villagers at gunpoint demanding to be shown where the Việt Minh had gone. Everyone was a suspect, even the children. It was easy for me to practice the neutrality that Thầy wished us to. I had seen horrors inflicted by both sides.

At lunchtime the crowds began to dissipate.

Hương stood up and picked up a gasoline can she had carried with her from the temple. I had not questioned her; often we would be offered gas or kerosene for the temple.

Then she cleared a small space and sat down in the lotus position. I knelt down to join her, and she shook her head.

"Please watch me. You have the letter to Thầy?"

Startled, I nodded.

Some of the curious began to gather around her. Hương had not meditated in the street before, and this was unusual.

Then her voice rang out across the street. "I do this to wish for peace," she smiled.

Suddenly she doused herself with kerosene from the gasoline can. She produced a lighter from her robe and snapped it alight.

Horrified, I started forward. But then flames enveloped Hương and the heat drove me back. Her silhouette blazed with fire and people came running out of their homes.

The familiar smell of burning flesh overwhelmed me. Tears streamed down my face as I clasped my hands together in prayer for her.

My eyes stung as I wept. My gaze was reluctantly drawn to the burning of her silhouette, calm in the lotus position. Her benevolence was gone. My innocence was gone.

Out of nowhere, or so it seemed to me, other brothers and sisters came, ringing a gong.

"A martyr is dead! A martyr is dead!"

People clustered around me in fascination. Someone took photographs, and a monk stood forward to burn incense. It was like a macabre festival.

The abbess put her hands on my shoulders. Coming to, I opened my eyes. The remains were hidden from view by the press of curious bodies.

"She has gone to the other shore. Her sacrifice will be noted for peace."

I turned to her stricken. "I didn't know ..."

"I know," the abbess said. She radiated calm, the same calm Hương had radiated moments before.

"I have a letter from her. To Thầy."

"Then you must send it to him," the abbess told me and gently escorted me aside.

"You can return to the temple today," she suggested to me. "Pray for her memory and for peace."

I returned to the place where we had slept side by side just the night before.

Weeping, I touched and stroked the floor where she had lain just hours ago as if by touching where she had been, I could be closer to where she had gone.

I sent the letter to Thầy, and I never knew if he received it or if he was able to respond.

When news of his permanent exile reached me, I wept again.

I am still weeping for Hương. And for peace.

NGHĨA,
LOVE OF COUNTRY

SOUTH VIETNAM, 1980

The past is in the present and is in the future.
Time passes with the historical dimension.
And experience is the ultimate dimension in time.
History is a wave and the ultimate dimension
is the water.

THÍCH NHẤT HẠNH

After Hương's death, the wars went on. The bombings did not stop. The press noted it as another Buddhist immolation. No one seemed to hear her cry except me. The SYSS tried to keep on with its work. Even when five volunteers were murdered in cold blood, we still continued to keep neutral and uphold Buddhist teachings.

It became too much for me. I retreated inside myself, though I prayed every day that Quan Âm would hear the cries of the wounded and make the wars stop. When the Communists won, with the Americans gone, I naively believed maybe now there would be peace.

Peace though was hard to manage under the Communist regime. The re-education camps began and even the Buddhists fell under suspicion.

When Thầy was prevented from returning to Vietnam, our worst fears were realised. The Buddhist Church was created, a state organisation with which all temples had to align themselves. Thầy's books and teachings were still banned so some went underground. Some hid in plain sight, aligning themselves with the Buddhist Church so they could go on practising openly.

I lived in fear after the fall of Saigon and found myself longing to return to the place of my origins. I still dreamt of a time of peace, where I was meditating openly under the watchful eye of Quan Âm. The tea plantations in my dreams were in the hills, and the buildings vast and modern.

Peace for the Buddhists had not come yet. Who would have guessed that the Communists would fear Buddhist influence and ban soup kitchens and large public gatherings?

Sometimes I had sensed déjà vu while meditating, of memories that did not quite fit. The dream reoccurred to me as if to mock me;

43

Vietnam was at peace but we had to hide our rituals in our homes and close the monastery doors to the public.

I decided to return to the coast, further away from Saigon, now Hồ Chí Minh City and wondered what I would find there. Maybe I could restore the graves of my ancestors from so long ago. Maybe other people from my village would return now that the wars were over. Maybe I could find another home by the sea.

There were many people moving after the war ended. Some headed towards the city, hoping for a better future. Others fled for the coast, knowing they didn't have a future in Vietnam. As a lone nun, I told strangers I was displaced from my fishing village and wanting to return there. The truth without finer details sufficed for me. They greeted my nun's robe with welcome and seldom did I have to beg for food; more often it was given to me without prompting in return for a blessing.

The horrors of my precognition had stopped after the fall of Saigon and I was only left with dreams of peace. Sometimes my dreams would be of meditating under siege, flashbacks I thought of finding mindfulness during wartime. Other times I flashbacked to Hương's immolation and awoke hot and burning.

In the daytime it was different. The countryside was wrecked by war, and the trees were only slowly beginning to grow back if at all. On my way back to my village I helped out the wounded where I could and prayed for them.

I began to dread what I was going to find on the coast. Maybe the village would be gone, with no signs at all. Maybe Agent Orange had poisoned the fields and the forests, leaving nothing I could recognise.

The reality was worse and better than my expectations. The sea was black and the sand filthy with oil. New villages had begun to spring up on the coast, and fishermen were still trying to draw catches from the sea and the rivers. But normal village life was returning, there was a market and here, far from the city, people still prayed in the open. Outside each shack were flowers and incense for the lunar month and children played by the riverside still.

I wondered whether I would find the people I had grown up with. Scattered after the Việt Minh invasion would they, like me, come back home?

I headed towards where our ancestors were buried. Old guilt gnawed at me, that I had not the courage to bury Bà all those years ago. The cemetery's fences were gone but someone had been taking care of the graves recently. I traced my way back to our family headstone from my fading memory. The headstone was mostly destroyed but the base still remained. In front of it, grass grew where the burial mound once stood. Trembling, I weeded the grass from around the plot. The last time I begged, I had received mandarins and I produced one for the dead.

Had Bà forgiven me for not attending to her memory as I should?

I have come home, I told the waiting sky and the hallowed ground. I will tend to you now. And to the memories of my family who did not survive or had gone missing.

I was lucky to be alive. I uttered a prayer to the dead and opened the mandarin for them to eat. My hands sticky with the juice, I bowed to my ancestors and wished them peace.

I paced slowly around the market, following where the bamboo perimeter fence had set the boundaries of our village. Someone had built a shack over where our house once stood. It jarred me seeing

45

strangers inhabiting the land where I grew up. Most of the familiar markers from my childhood had been destroyed. I had come back to find nothing.

Only at night, orienting by the stars, could I get a sense of where the village đình had been. Tears cascaded down my face as I retraced my steps back to where Bà must have died. It was just outside the marketplace and another old woman snuffled in the dark at my presence.

"*Chao chị.* Hello sister. What are you remembering?"

"My family died here," I murmured through my tears and wiped my face with the back of my hand.

"Ah. Do you have anyone left?"

"No."

"How unlucky. I have one son still alive. He fishes and looks after me. I do not remember you, but many of us fled during the American War. I used to live five miles from here before the wars. Now we are lucky we are still alive, heh?"

I nodded in the darkness at the old woman's pragmatism.

"Come sleep here," the old woman said companionably. "I'm Bình."

"Liên," I introduced myself and made my way over to where she was sitting, under a plastic tarpaulin.

When the morning light came, I saw the face of my new friend. Creased with experience, her eyes were still bright in the dawn and shrewd, taking in my clothes and well-worn hands. Her own hands were busy, sorting out fishing nets with practiced fingers. Hesitantly I joined her. My fingers remembered how, although my mind did not.

"You are from the sea," she nodded her approval at my handiwork as we laid one net aside. Her son, Hiếu, a tall lanky boy with a limp, took the net and headed towards the water. I could see the bones of his back through paper-thin skin, but he still retained a little strength, I thought.

We talked around what we truly wished to know about each other, whether one was with the Communists or not. I proclaimed myself a Buddhist and saw sisterly recognition in her eyes. But she still maintained a distance from me, which I respected. In those days, no one really knew who to trust.

Then a strange thing occurred. Another woman came up to us and inclined her head in respect. She offered Bình rice cakes and then Bình gestured for her to give one to me.

"Liên, my friend," she said as if by explanation and the woman left without asking for payment or anything in return. I began to wonder. Was Bình like Bà, the keeper of the village đình?

But my questions were set aside when I smelt the cooked rice as Bình opened the banana leaf wrappings of the cakes. Hungrily I untangled the string around the cake, and anticipated the first mouthful of fish and rice. As I tasted the fish and its familiar strong flavourings from the coast, tears came to my eyes. I had come home.

"Good, heh? She is the best cook around here."

"*Cam on chi*, thank you sister," I said, my hands sticky with the glutinous rice.

She smiled.

"When I was younger we used to worship the Lady of the Realm close to here," I said after my hunger was sated.

"Ah yes. I remember a story about the Lady before the wars. She blessed a virgin girl with warnings of the wars, and the girl and some of the villagers that listened to the warning escaped when the Northerners came. If only the Lady had warned the entire country."

I felt myself reddening. I had never heard of my story told like this and I felt alien to myself being described as a virginal girl again. Yet the story was not told about how my family was killed. I was able to help some but not others, the curse of my gift.

"I do not understand why the Communists have banned her worship."

Bình turned her shrewd gaze on me and I felt myself being assessed and weighed up in her mind.

"The Lady is for women. We are not a threat," I continued.

"Hồ Chí Minh is a jealous master," Bình said as we were interrupted by a man who approached us. His clothes were in disrepair and in worse condition than my own. Yet he bowed to Bình and discreetly gave her a wad of crinkled dirty notes. The money disappeared quickly through Bình's hands and the man went away without acknowledging my presence as if ashamed.

"I save my worship for the *dong*. Money. It will get me out of trouble in a way that faith cannot," she said firmly and the subject was closed.

Yet later in the day as we walked to the beach to help bring in what little catch there was, she pulled me aside before we reached the water. "There is a tall stone that some of the faithful visit every now and again, where the Lady is said to have given dreams to the virginal girl. It is in the barren forest area. I'll take you there later."

48

I smiled for the first time since Saigon fell. The spirits were still with the people regardless of Communist demands. Hope, absent for so long from my heart, began to grow again.

To my surprise we did not gut the fish ourselves, but gave that dirty work to the woman who had presented us with rice cakes earlier that day. Her son retreated to the tarpaulin to sleep as the heat began to bake the afternoon. I was sleepy and wished to nap too, but Bình pulled at my arm to keep walking.

"No one watches in the middle of the day," she explained as she led me away from the market towards the barren forest.

A lone bird wailed wheeling far up in the sky, and my memories of how the forest used to be brought more tears to my eyes. The smell of ash filled my hair and nostrils as we walked. Amongst the stumps and burnt out trunks of trees, new growth was beginning slowly, little green tendrils reaching for the air among the ruins.

We came across the rock outcropping suddenly. It was hidden among the remains of trees. Someone had cleared the rocks of ash, and a wilting purple paper garland hung around the tallest standing stone.

A sensory memory of sleeping here in the sun, Tài by my side, came to me. My skin tingled with the remembrance of safety and peace. This time I did not cry, but felt warmth, remembering that once I had felt like this.

Bình bowed to the tallest rock outcropping and I followed suit. Then we sat on one of the other rocks just like I had so long ago.

"I wanted peace so much," Bình reflected after we shared a companionable silence. "But I did not imagine it would be like this."

It was the closest she had come to saying anything about the Communists.

"Neither did I," I replied, my mouth dry and full of ash. Bà would not have wanted the Lady hidden away like this.

I stood up again, heedless of what Bình thought, and stood in front of the garlanded rock, my hands in prayer. I felt my soul settle as I focused on the image of the Lady in my mind. She merged seamlessly with Quan Âm at that moment. The goddesses were with me.

I did not know what I wished for then. But when I opened my eyes, I saw Bình observing me.

"You were a monastic," she said.

I nodded. Bình got to her feet and began to walk back down the slope.

"The people will remember," she said as I joined her.

Even hidden away the Lady could still bring hope, I thought. I had found the Lady in many guises, but the strongest seemed to be the Lady I had inside.

It was through Bình that I found the future again. More people gave her money and goods. When she invited me to join a money-lending circle with a laugh, I realised what she was.

"I know you have nothing," she said when I declined. She was a money-lender, a profession that was looked down on, but deemed necessary in these times.

Owing her nothing meant I could truly be her friend. I did not ask how she survived the wars, it was evident in her shrewdness and knowledge of the black market. She also dealt in food coupons as well as cash, and I never enquired as to where the coupons came from.

One day she presented me with a badly photocopied book.

"I thought you might like this," she said. It was *Lotus in a Sea of Fire* by Thích Nhất Hạnh, well-worn and handled. I bowed in gratitude.

The village rebuilt itself, but without the village đình. Houses sprang up but where the village đình once stood there was an empty place for the market and the children to play in. Bình arranged for a house to be built for herself and her son, and once it was completed invited me to stay with her as a guest.

A loudspeaker was installed where the latest Communist messages were broadcast and the occasional Communist cadre would visit the village for a time then go back to the city. Bình gleaned that the cadres viewed visiting the coastal villages as a chore and did not wish to be stationed there.

Then Bình began trafficking in people. The first I knew of it was when strange families would come to the village and disappear the next day. In those fearful times, no one asked too many questions. Ever alert, I wondered whether Bình knew anything about it. But this time the wily money-lender did not confide in me.

I went to visit the rock outcropping and noticed new offerings, marigolds and little bean cakes from the city. I knelt by the rocks and prostrated myself before the Lady, hoping that she had taken care of her worshippers.

That night I dreamt of Bình down at the beach at night with her son. They were pushing a fishing boat out to sea, in an eerie echo of what had happened to me so long ago. The fishing boat was jammed full of strange people, mothers with children and fathers with grim faces.

I woke up with sweat on my brow and salt on my lips. Bình and her son were nowhere to be seen in the darkness of our shared house. I knew better than to try and find them on the beach. Bình would not appreciate that.

The next morning, Bình looked weary. Her son had dragged himself into the house and had fallen asleep in his clothes. Rumours at the market said another communist cadre was coming with soldiers, news that Bình barely blinked at. With a heavy sigh, she sipped her coffee with condensed milk.

"Liên, do you ever wish to leave Vietnam? Go out of the Communist reach to America?"

I noticed her gaze on me and I realised that she was not asking lightly. Somehow she had the means to get there.

"No," I said automatically. Then I thought a little more. "This is my country and my home."

The Lady resides here, was my unspoken thought, but I knew Bình would not be sympathetic to that.

"Hmmmm." Bình replied and was lost in thought. "I do not hear from the ones that escape. It's a long way over the sea to Malaysia. And what would I do in the land of white ghosts? Here I am rich with a house and a son with business." She laughed, a sour laugh and I did not join in.

My dreams of peace, of meditating outside in the open, seem even more remote now. My tears have receded into a sitting sadness and a happy joy that somehow I am still alive.

I had lost so much, my village destroyed and yet my ancestral land is still here. In the shelter of Bình's networks I was safe, yet the communist regime kept me awake with one eye open.

They had forced our worship behind closed doors, with family altars hiding inside. When I do mindful breathing, walking and exercises from the monastery, I do it away from prying eyes. I valued Bình all the more because I could trust her – a rare privilege in those days.

Every day I sat beside Bình in the marketplace and watched people come and go. They grew familiar but not close to me. Most were displaced fisher people from further down south. The communist cadres, a pair of them, both men, walked amongst us briefly for an hour each morning then retreated to their office to drink beer and watch women.

I missed the people of my village, and every day I offered a prayer inside the house: may they be well wherever they may be.

METTA, LOVING KINDNESS
SOUTH VIETNAM, 1991

Touching the present moment,
we realize that the present is made of the past
and is creating the future.

THÍCH NHẤT HẠNH

One day a stranger came to the marketplace. I heard about him before I saw him physically, he claimed to be from the Lady of the Realm village. He was immediately directed to me and Bình and was accompanied by an inquisitive fisher woman.

"*Bác Liên*, Aunt Liên," the fisher woman greeted me.

I stared at the man in shock and peered into his matured features.

"Tai?"

"*Chị Liên*! Sister Liên!" His voice was rough and deep from smoking, and his deeply browned face was wrinkled. But when he embraced me in a hug, I finally knew we had returned home.

Bình graciously allowed us to sit in her lounge room to catch up on the years apart without prying villagers hanging on every word. I could not stop smiling, I was so happy. Tài walked with a limp but his dark eyes still sparkled mischievously. I wondered how I appeared to him, with wrinkled hands and eyes, stooped over from catching fish. But the years seemed to dissolve when he smiled at me and caught my eye.

"How did you survive?" I asked after making him a cup of tea.

He became sober as he sipped his tea slowly.

"I was taken away with your mother and sister to help infiltrate the strategic hamlets." He opened his hands, rough with years of hard work and calluses. "Your mother and sister died early on of pneumonia during the wet season. They did not have a strong enough will to live."

The guardedness in his eyes relaxed when I indicated the small family shrine that Bình kept in an alcove in the kitchen. No Communist cadre would have superstitious rubbish in his home.

"I had a wife and child. They were killed during the wars," he said.

"So you took vows?" he asked a little later.

I hesitated. Suddenly I did not want to be a monastic to Tài.

"I'm not actively linked to a temple anymore. Nowadays you can't be."

"No you can't." He fell silent, looking at me with a frank open gaze and a smile on his lips.

The moment deepened and I remembered how he used to be with me all those years ago before I became a woman. He must have been remembering the same time for his next words hit my heart.

"Do you still dream, Liên?"

"Yes. I dreamt of the wars and people dying. But I always had this vision of peace." I found myself telling him of my hopeful dream, which I had not shared with anyone since Hương died.

"I hope that time will come," he said seriously. "Although I cannot see it now."

Tears came to my eyes, at all the times we had both lost thanks to the Việt Minh. We should not have been parted.

He grasped my hand, and held it as I wiped away my tears. I had never felt so old until that moment.

"And you never had a husband or children?"

I shook my head.

We ended up in an embrace. It seemed the most natural thing to do in the world.

I showed Tài our family graves and how I had cleaned his family plot as well. I was proud that the flowers I had laid at both sites were still fresh and the thanks I received from him made me blush.

"All this time I was praying for my ancestors. And you were looking after them for me, little Liên."

I nodded.

"I'm glad I've returned and you are here. Is no one else here?"

Mutely I shook my head, and tears threatened again.

"I'm glad that most of the men died here where they were born, rather than being forced into slavery." He shuddered and looked off into the distance, into memories I could not reach.

We knelt at my family's plot and prostrated ourselves before leaving some mandarin pieces with the flowers for the graves. Then, holding hands, we began to walk back to Bình's house.

I noticed the tension in the marketplace and the silence first. Even Tài picked up that something was amiss. There were no sounds of gossip or lively chatter. I glanced around. Bình's son was awake, a rare enough sight during the daytime, and was busy fixing a net with his head down.

He did not acknowledge me.

I felt a prickle down my back and turned around. Tài let go of my hand.

A new communist cadre, young and fresh from Hanoi surveyed me and Tài.

"Are you married?" he rapped out impatiently.

"We are," Tài lied and my heart swelled with joy.

"No one at the office informed me about you two. You have to come with me and register at the office."

Tai and I looked at each other and reluctantly followed his instructions. I grasped quickly that the cadres Bình had bribed were no longer in charge. And Bình was nowhere to be seen.

I had never been inside the hot concrete box that the communist cadres claimed as their office. The new Vietnamese flag hung limply in front of it, red with a yellow star.

We stepped inside the office. A fan was blowing and the two other cadres were alert at their desks. Books and records were collected behind them in untidy piles. Their customary bottles of beer were nowhere to be seen.

"Who are these two?"

"*Chị Liên*. Sister Liên. *Anh Tài*. Brother Tài."

"How come they are married and not in the register books?"

Silence fell except for the blowing of the rickety fan.

"This is why we are inspecting all the outposts in the south. You cannot allow people to just appear in your jurisdiction. They may be trying to escape."

He glanced back at us, and I said nothing, breathing in and out to calm my panic.

Where was Bình?

"You. Anh Tài. How do you serve your country?"

" My first wife and children died in the American War. I came back here, to my village, to pay honour to my ancestors and return to fishing."

"You should not indulge this sort of superstitious crap," the cadre from the North chided the other two. "But fishing is a good occupation and suitable work. Chị Liên. You are from the market, yes?"

I nodded, my palms sweating. What did he want?

"Where is Chị Bình?"

"She went to the next village to trade," I lied, hoping that I was not hanging myself and Bình in the process.

"They are respectable traders," one of the other cadres suddenly said, in loyalty to his bribes. "Her son is in the market if you want information about her."

"I see. Anh Tài and Chị Liên. Your loyalty now is to the party that liberated you from the puppet forces. Not to your ancestors or your village. Your loyalty is for your fellow comrades. I expect to see you at the village meeting tonight."

He dismissed us with a wave of his hand.

We scuttled out the door and quickly returned to Bình's empty house. Once safely inside Tài locked the door.

"Where is Bình?" Tài asked. He had seen through my lie.

"I don't know," I said truthfully. I was scared. I did not know whether Bình's bribes would work on a young fervent Communist or whether she would end up in prison.

"I did not come back South for this," Tài said to me angrily. "I had heard in the South they were more lax."

"They usually are," I told him miserably. I was now beginning to realise how influential Bình was in the village.

"What do they do at these village meetings?" he asked me.

"Usually they get the children to sing songs to Hồ Chí Minh. Nothing more than that. We are too poor and uneducated to be sent to a camp."

"I see. Liên …" he looked at me strangely and I wondered what he was thinking.

"Liên, I did not come back only for my ancestors. I heard that for a fee, you can be smuggled by fishing boat out to the ocean to Malaysia. Do you know anything about this?"

I nearly laughed out loud from nervousness.

"No I don't," I lied. When Bình returned, I would suggest him as a customer to her. If she returned.

"Would you leave me so soon?" I asked lightly.

"I would want you to come with me," he said seriously.

Stunned, I could only swallow at his suggestion. My ancestors were here. Bà was here.

And one day, peace would come. Or would it?

I had begun to doubt my own prescience, I had held on to that dream for years and it was still no closer to being fulfilled.

"Think about it, Liên." He drew me close and I smelt his cigarettes on his breath and sweat. But still it was comforting when he put his arms around me and kissed me on the hair.

The rest of the day, the village was tense as the new cadre made himself known. Everyone turned up early for the village meeting, no one wanted to be accused of being laggard.

The straggly choir of fisher children were waving new red flags and their piping voices sang to Uncle Ho as the cadres made their way to the centre of the marketplace.

The new cadre opened the proceedings with a speech about how Uncle Ho had benefitted the people. Then he denounced those who helped people escape to foreign shores and how the village would be rewarded if the people smugglers were turned in.

During his speech, Bình suddenly appeared behind me and Tài, with her son. She was carrying a bag of candies and tobacco from town. When the speech finished, she bobbed her head up and down, looking like another serene old woman. She stumbled and walked slowly over to the communist cadres and gave them all wrapped red presents. Then she distributed the candies to the children and the tobacco to the men with her son's help.

The new cadre did not open his present. I prayed that Bình had not put a customary bribe in the present. Then Bình returned to my side with her son.

"Cousin," she greeted me and Tài formally. To the new cadre's eyes, she seemed to be just another peasant trying to please. But to the villagers, she was someone reminding them of her ability to gift them with her money. Bình, I was discovering, was the real village head not the communist cadres posted far from Hanoi.

When the village meeting broke up with all the adults and children singing the national anthem, I finally was able to smile at Bình and be glad of her return.

Bình and her son resumed fishing with Tài's and my assistance over the next few days. It was after Bình had warmed to Tài that I surreptitiously mentioned to her his interest in her smuggling operation.

"You trust this man?" Bình asked me seriously and I nodded.

"It cannot be now. Maybe a month or two from now. When the new cadre will either stay or leave."

The wily, cautious woman would not even talk about the smuggling in detail in front of me.

Tai sighed when I told him that the smuggling network was dormant until the cadre left.

"I did not think it would be easy," he said.

"I don't know if I will go with you," I said tentatively. I told him all the horror stories that I had heard from Bình's son. Only one or two of those who had left by boat had been heard of again by people in Vietnam. There were pirates, and many people died at sea.

"I don't know if I can risk my life. Having been close to dying so many times already."

"I feel dead being here," Tài tried to explain to me. "I cannot do well like your friend Bình living a duplicitous life. Wondering who is going to inform on me so I will be forced to go to a re-education camp instead of them. Don't you wish to be somewhere that you can worship openly? Maybe your peace is overseas not here."

I fell mute. I could not tell him that I had not dreamed of him one way or the other. All my recent dreams were of peace, and I was certain it was in Vietnam. The Lady had blessed me and I had to stay and make sure she was not forgotten in our village.

It was the only topic in which we would halt conversation, in a growing unease that some day we would be parted.

Finally the day came when Bình offered Tài a passage on a fishing boat. She only gave him a day's notice, which gave me less than 24 hours to grieve.

"Are you sure you will not come with me, Liên?" He only asked me one more time, as I knotted a banana leaf rice cake for him to take on the trip.

"Are you sure you will not stay?" I asked, but he was silent.

"I will contact you as soon as I can," he said. "You know they are going to come looking for me."

I gave him a thin smile. "I will wail into their ears that no man can be trusted with your heart. That you have run away with a younger woman to the city. That you have deserted me." Although I did not intend it, on the last sentence I felt a pang of truth.

We held each other close in those last few hours, and I treasured his solid presence. His love for me had restored my faith in the goodness of the human heart. That I understood why he had to go made it all the more painful.

"Liên, you have always been in my mind and my — "

I put a finger on my lips. I did not want to hear a romantic lie in my last moments with him. He had loved his wife and children and he had thought me dead. Just like I had thought of him, and had tried to replace him with others in my heart.

When Bình's son came to accompany him, I could not help the tears that welled up in my eyes. I could see that Tài too was trying not to cry in front of another man.

We embraced one last time and then let each other go.

MAITREYA,
TRUE LOVE

SOUTH VIETNAM, 2007

I have arrived, I am home.
In the here and in the now.

THÍCH NHẤT HẠNH

It took another decade before word reached the village that foreigners were being let into the country again. I had found some measure of peace, praying to the Lady and meditating next to the stone monolith that looked out onto the village. Bình was right. She grew more prosperous even under the Communist eye. Somehow she was lucky and was never caught. I doubted it was just luck, though; she knew all the Communist cadres by name and never failed to give them gifts.

I helped her with the money lending but she never let me into the ins and outs of her people smuggling business. This way, you cannot speak if you are taken in, she said to me when I once offered to help.

I aged slowly with the quiet days weaving in and out. Every night I thanked the Lady that I was whole and untouched, and I lived to see another day. I heard and saw pictures of Hồ Chí Minh City with wealth beyond imagining. Some of the young people of the village went there to seek their fortunes. But I was never tempted. Seeing the first mopeds come into the village was enough, and white ghosts with backpacks carefree and light sans responsibility. The television in Bình's house showed me prosperity in the world outside the village. White ghosts populated some of the programs and I learned that they had love stories much like our own.

As the years went by, I stopped waiting for Tài to contact me. There was no way of contacting him if he had survived the trip to Malaysia. Bình promised to inform me of news, but she had rarely heard of whether the trips she had organised had been successful or not. They all knew that contacting her would be the prelude to her being investigated by the communist cadres.

Then one day I heard that Thích Nhất Hạnh was being allowed to visit the country and do public dharma talks.

"After suppressing the Buddhists for so long, why?" I asked, fearing it was a trap to assassinate the Zen Master who resided in France.

"He is going to perform Great Ceremonies of Mourning for those who have suffered during the wars from all sides," Bình told me, as she split a pumpkin seed with her teeth.

I shook my head in disbelief. This opening of religious freedom from the government was too good to be true.

Bình gave me a flyer with Thầy's tour dates and told her son to take me to Saigon.

Hồ Chí Minh City had outgrown itself over the decades. The foreign neon signs and the density of all the people on mopeds and bicycles overwhelmed me. Bình's son Hiếu was at ease with all this wealth, he talked on his mobile phone while riding his motorcycle. It was only his filial piety to his mother that kept him in the village, he told me. That and frequent 'business' trips to Hồ Chí Minh City. When we arrived, he had to show me the central shopping district with foreign Western brands and shopping malls. I blinked in the light of this extravagance and marvelled at the carefree youth with their foreign clothes, fashions and gadgets.

Was this what peace and prosperity looked like? Hiếu bragged to me that Western cities were like Hồ Chí Minh City. Wide, clean pavements and shops glistening behind clean plate-glass windows.

Then we encountered a build up of parked mopeds and buses blocking the roads. It was like a festival with flower sellers and food vendors mingling around the crush of the crowd.

"Thầy is speaking in there," Hiếu pointed somewhere in the middle of the crowds. He parked his motorcycle and we began to weave in and out of the crush of people. Speakers and lights were rigged up along the road and the glare of white reflected off the expectant people's faces. A vendor with pirated copies of Thầy's books brushed past us as Hiếu pushed his way further into the crowd. Sweat soaked my best plain white shirt and pants. The people were hemmed in so closely together, it made me dizzy.

Finally Hiếu had to stop when the masses of people refused to give way to him. In front of us was the giant stage set out on the road glittering in the spotlights. Gold umbrellas framed where Thầy was going to sit, and behind him were monks and nuns dressed in brown from Plum Village. They were standing, their hands clasped in prayer. A bell sounded and the people around us rustled for a better view as Thầy slowly proceeded through the crowds, gladioli flowers waving in the wake of his passing. I could not see much but I shared the crowd's anticipation and awe as he ascended to the dais where he was to speak.

The Zen Master was still youthful at eighty years old, his bald head shiny and his presence radiating peace. Then the monks and nuns began to chant Avoliketera's name, accompanying the tears sliding down my cheeks.

Nam Mô A Di Đà. Nam Mô A Di Đà. Nam Mô A Di Đà

In his dharma talk that day, Thầy spoke about family and our ancestors, which brought more tears to my eyes. He spoke about anger and how we needed to cradle our anger like a baby, and practice loving speech and deep listening for those we loved. Loneliness crept into my being as I found myself thinking of Tài and how he had left. But as the nuns and monks sang, I felt energy inside myself rise and take wing.

There was talk that Prajna Monastery in Bát Nhả was now open to the public. People were able to worship openly and young people were flocking to join the temple. Thầy was going to do a public retreat there, the monastics said. So I followed Thầy's tour from Saigon to Bát Nhả in a crowded public bus. I left Bình's son to go back home and tell his mother where I had gone. Although she did not believe, I thought the money-lender would understand.

When we came upon Prajna Monastery in the embrace of some small hills, I felt memory fall into place. The gates loomed above us and as we walked in, I saw a gorgeous white meditation hall with wide windows looking out onto tea plantations on the hills.

Excitement stirred within me. Was this the site of what I had dreamed about for so long?

People milled around me while monastics staffed tables with laptop computers, registering people for the retreat. The joy of the crowd was infectious, this sort of public teaching was rarely allowed. Even the obvious presence of communist cadres scattered through the crowd in cheap blue suits was not enough to quell people's enthusiasm.

Books were being sold and enterprising photographers sold pictures of the Zen Master from his public talks in Saigon. Though the crowd numbered thousands, I felt safe among them in a way I had never felt before. It was as if mindfulness had affected us all.

Present moment, wonderful moment.

I decided to explore the monastery. Stepping on the paving stones I wandered under the shadows of young pine trees down the slope to find a giant statue of Quan Âm sitting on top of a miniature lake. Monastics and lay people were clustered around the white stone statue chatting quietly. My memories of my dreams shifted and stirred.

This was close, but not identical, to the dream I'd had for so long. Already the peace and hope that threatened to overwhelm me was cracking through my reserve. After all the suffering, maybe now the Communists were at peace enough to allow the nation's spirit to shine again.

I wandered down the hill. The slope of the tea plantations was familiar to my eye. I followed two novices with their shaved heads and brown robes strolling along a winding path. I passed by two large white halls, with bright mosaics of the Buddha and animals – clean and modern.

The peace and tranquillity touched an old chord in me from when I was a monastic during the American War. But this time, the skies were clear and the people around me unwounded.

I have arrived, I am home.

The path followed the slope to the river. I looked to my left and there was the white-seated Buddha statue of my dream almost hidden by the trees looking over to the tea plantations.

Tears streamed down my face as I stumbled down to the river. A wooden bridge went across it to a wooden gazebo. I found a rock to sit on. I did not meditate at first but slowly breathed in and out as I felt the rightness of the scenery settle around me.

I had dreamed of peace. And finally it had come when the Communists opened the doors to their old perceived enemies, foreigners and Thích Nhất Hạnh. I was old now. But Quan Âm had heard my prayers.

Na-mo A-vo- li-ke-te-ra. Na-mo A-vo- li-ke-te-ra.

In Prajna Monastery, I dared to hope that peace is possible. The government allowed Thích Nhất Hạnh, the exiled Zen Master, to come to teach the people and publish his books. Perhaps the government had finally realised the spirit of the people and Buddhist liberation is no threat to them. And even foreigners have taken to the fruit of the practice. Their white faces mirror our calm and their joy is like the spring from the river. When we sing of the island, the inner island of peace that we return to, it is my turn to weep.

Present moment, wonderful moment.

I like to return to my island.

Our teacher Thầy says, though we have suffered at the hands of the foreigners, they were once children too and we can feel compassion for the suffering children the invaders once were.

Form is emptiness, emptiness is form.

Gate, gate, paragate, parasamgate bodhi svaha.

Gone, gone to the other shore. All Hail!

There are Americans and French laypeople from the international Plum Village *sangha* who accompany Thầy on his visit. Their faces shine with mindfulness like the monks and nuns. One American man, tall and large approaches me and apologises for America's involvement in the war with tears in his eyes.

I cannot hate these people or even fear them. When Thầy says the Great Ceremonies he conducts are for all that suffered during the wars, I believe him. At first I could not believe that Westerners would believe in Buddhist practice. But now when I see them sitting cross-legged and meditating, standing up for the monks and nuns, and breathing mindfully in and out, I see the Buddha within them.

I have arrived, I am home.

During the morning walking meditation I feel myself smile at the stillness permeating through the young pine forest of the Prajna Monastery grounds.

I am calm like the lake.

I am solid as the mountain.

When Thầy says we all inter-be and inter-are, and I see foreigners holding the hands of the Vietnamese congregation, I understand the Heart Sutra at last.

We all inter-be and inter-are. Our enemy is not other humans but fear and anger.

When I reach inside myself and meditate on compassion for the poor children the northerners once were, something inside me dissolves. I am free, I am free.

How can I continue to hate the American War veteran who cried in my arms for what he had done? The Việt Minh man who raped me so long ago, was a child too once. He had been brutalised by being a soldier in the wars.

I have let go of my fear, like used clothing.

I take incense and mandarins down to the giant Quan Âm statue and prostrate myself at her feet. The Lady is so powerful that she reaches even into the hearts of foreigners. I feel her embrace around me in the kindness and openness of all these people.

I am too old to join the Plum Village *sangha* in France with Thầy. But I become another one of the old women monastics tending to Prajna Monastery, feeding Communist cadres, foreigners and lay people alike.

Vietnam has found peace, and I have finally found peace inside through compassion for others. Quan Âm, Avoliketera and the Lady have shown me the way through Thầy.

Thầy talks about continuation – how we all are the seeds from our ancestors.

Bà is still alive in me and tears come to my eyes. Though I am far from my village, I feel the love of all of those who have held me close, my family, Tài and the easy acceptance of Bình, my benefactor. With this *sangha* I am never alone, I tell myself.

Compassion for all those who have suffered and who have created suffering for me, runs through my tired bones. Energised, I come slowly to my feet, clasp my hands and bow my head to the Lady.

I am free, I am free, I am free.

KARUNA, COMPASSION

PRAJNA MONASTERY, SOUTH VIETNAM, 2009

This body is not me; I am not caught in this body,
I am life without boundaries, I have never been born
and I have never died.

THÍCH NHẤT HẠNH

The sound of the bell returns me to my true home. Opening my eyes, I return from the depths of meditation, as if from underwater, from the ocean. The bell echoes in the hollow of my soul and beyond. I look down at wrinkled brown hands with prominent blue veins, once they were smooth as the marble of a goddess statue. Memories of lives, past lives, begin to surface and I ask my mind to be still.

Breathing in, I am breathing in.

Breathing out, I am breathing out.

The sound of the bell penetrates my mind. Easing my posture, I let go of my memories, which floats to the top of my thoughts like a leaf on a pond.

I am fresh, fresh as a flower.

I am still, still as a mountain.

Glass shatters and a ripple runs through the consciousness of the meditating monks and nuns. The hired mobs are back again. A rumour is whispered that the authorities in Bát Nhà have paid villagers up to 150 kilometres away to come and destroy the monastery. I consciously breathe out my tension, trying to release my fear. In the middle of the *sangha*, circled by three hundred of my brothers and sisters, the practice is strong in the meditation hall. The terracotta Buddha statue at the front of the hall is still intact, though the white walls are filthy and desecrated with piss. In a brown nun's robe, I feel visible, old and vulnerable. I attempt to return back to the island of peace and calm within, breathing in and out.

Na-mo Avo-li-ke-te-ra. Na-mo Avo-li-ke-te-ra.

We sing her name, Avoliketera, Quan Âm, the goddess of mercy, she who hears the cries of the world. In the courtyard of the temple, there was a white marble statue of her, holding a vase of water, her hand in a *mudra*. I dread to think what the mobs have done to her.

I have called her name in many guises, as the Lady of the Realm, as Mary the mother of God. I do not know if she has ever heard me.

The smell of incense infuses my robe and I return again to the peace within.

I feel the menace of the men surrounding us and feel sick in the stomach. We have been without water and electricity and much food for the past few months. Our practice shone brighter as we starved and took comfort from each other's presence. But my fear has been nibbling at my peace, and I have wanted to run again. Breathing in, I try and cradle my fear like a child, soothing myself. I feel vulnerable as a nun in a drab brown robe; the men have leered at all of us.

Sanctuaries are an illusion, only suffering is real. I know that this is not what the Buddha taught, and my experience has made my own sayings out of his teachings. I believe that any safety I find is temporary, any refuge is not permanent. But my teacher would say, all things are impermanent and change. I hope that our situation will change. Some days I cannot bear another moment of being under siege.

When I meditate, my monkey mind replays memories, of times before when I have starved and begged for food. I try to let the memories go, flow through me back to the past where they belong. Then I am able to meditate truly, on the here and now in the present moment.

The rain falls in a steady drumming on the roof of the meditation hall. I catch myself swaying gently. Dizziness claims me for a moment and I open my eyes. More men have come into the hall, this time carrying crowbars and hammers. Some have a different look to them, and a shudder runs down my spine as they methodically start banging at the meditation hall walls with their tools. Police, I suspect, as they do not have the disorder and violent randomness of the other men. Having no other enemy to turn on, the Vietnamese now turn on themselves.

Today time is transparent to me and I can move in and out of my memories as my consciousness tries to resume its stillness. Bad memories emerge and I try not to get caught up with them like the tide. To follow those thoughts would hook me back into the past. I try to sit back and observe from a place of calm.

From my island inside myself I touch the roots of my suffering, live like a throbbing wound.

I retreat to the practice inside itself to release my anger and fear. Fear and anger are the enemy of mankind and the Communists are afraid of the Buddhists, like President Diem once was.

Breathing in, I touch my fear.

Breathing out, I release my fear.

The loudspeaker messages are stronger now, interrupting our meditation, denouncing Thích Nhất Hạnh and ordering us to return home. Paid by the authorities to drive us out of our home, the villagers harass the younger nuns. My breath is ragged and I calm myself breathing in and out. It reminds me too much of when my village was taken by the Việt Minh. I hear rumours that Vietnam

83

is now the chair of the Security Council of the UN. Two monastics from America came here and witnessed what was going on and then our water supply was destroyed. We are hoping the US Embassy will come and visit and see for themselves the destruction of our home. The smell of smoke permeates the hall, from the fires lit outside.

We have been warned. Why? The question is asked and word filters through the monastics that the last time Thích Nhất Hạnh visited Vietnam, he asked for the religious police to be disbanded. He is too popular, a sister whispers. In the few years that Prajna has been open to the public, many thousands of young people have come, many to become monastics.

The seeds of violence have been watered in these people. I am frightened but I try not to act from my fear.

Fear and anger are the enemy, not humanity.

As the rain pours down, more men enter the meditation hall. The wind and rain blows in the broken windows. We are ordered to stand up and move. There are many of them, three times as many as us. We are pushed and shoved. The most senior of us stands up and nods for us to obey. Frightened, I follow my sisters as we are expelled into the pouring rain.

Outside the destruction becomes apparent. Only the rain stops the fires that have burned down the walls of the nunnery and Buddha Hall. The statue of a woman holding the hands of two children are now armless and the children have been beheaded. The Avoliketera Quan Âm statue has been demolished to a pile of rubble. Stumps and broken tree trunks litter where we used to do walking meditation. The ground is churned up by thousands of feet and the smell of petrol is in the air. We are herded out of the Prajna gates, leaving our home behind.

Then the mob leaves us standing in the rain and returns to the monastery with their hammers and axes to destroy what remains.

"Go to Phước Huệ Temple in Bảo Lộc." The suggestion spreads and we begin to walk, then run into the rain. Mud squelches between my toes and I am drenched as we hurry towards sanctuary fifteen kilometres away. Behind us, the security police line the road urging us away from the monastery. I stumble on into the darkness, my hope destroyed.

Phước Huệ Temple is small, a miniature set of rectangular buildings, compared to the spacious monastery we have left behind. Their monastics hurriedly welcome us in to their main hall. We sit together jammed up and the smells of sweat and damp penetrate our being.

Nam Mô A Di Đà – Nam Mô A Di Đà – Nam Mô A Di Đà

Someone whispers Avoliketera's name in a sing-song chant and we all join in. The last time we sang this joyfully we were clustered around the ornamental lake in Prajna. Today the chant is a cry for help and mercy. Outside we hear the roar of police trucks and the growing sounds of the crowd.

We are blasted with orders over loudspeakers to leave the temple and return to our hometowns. Prajna was my home.

The abbot is asked to expel us, but he refuses. He is threatened with the destruction of the temple.

Then a message comes from the Catholic Church. They have offered sanctuary if we cannot stay in the temple. Outside one or

85

two of us have connected to the internet and used mobiles to make our plight public. Small hope kindles in me at the tentative smiles of the younger monastics. Someone begins singing about the island home inside the self.

I like to return to my island.

Then one of the older monastics ventures in from the outside.
He bears food from concerned villagers in Bảo Lộc. And a message from Thích Nhất Hạnh himself.

"Prajna is now legend. You carry the seeds of Prajna inside you to spread to the world."

Blinking back more tears I recollect the running of the waterfall down my spine and the calm of the white-seated Buddha statue that used to watch us walk beside the creek. Unbidden, the white serene face of the statue of Quan Âm's smile surfaces in my consciousness before disappearing.

I have prayed to the goddess outside of myself for so long. Now with my home destroyed and the police baying outside for us to leave, I have to find sanctuary inside myself again.

With the strength of the *sangha,* I retreat within and meditate once more. The sense of no self and the interconnectedness of all things emerge from me again. We inter-be and inter-are.

I remember a time of peace and what has been annihilated can grow again, as strong as our practice. What has happened once can happen again. Peace is still possible. Thầy has said it, Prajna is now legend inside us.

I remember this as the final deadline is read out. By New Year's Eve, we have to leave the temple and surrender to the police.

The small hands of my sisters find mine in the siege and instead of despair at their grasping, I find strength in their practice.

So we will disappear. My dreams now destroyed, I decide to accompany the monastics who will flee to Thailand.

I hug my sisters one by one, offering them comfort.

Like little brown sparrows, we disappear one by one into the night. I bow to the senior monastics one last time, a profound stillness settling over us all. Then I take off my monastic's robe and surrender it to them, to shuffle off into darkness.

ACKNOWLEDGEMENTS

My deepest thanks and gratitude to Thích Nhất Hạnh, the Plum Village Sangha, Present Moment Sangha, Green Bamboo Sangha and the Hanoi Community of Mindful Living for showing me the way. Thank you to Julia Byford and Ian Roberts for keeping the practice in the here and now, your inspiration and wisdom has been invaluable.

Thank you to Gail Jones for all her guidance and support, Melinda Jewell and the University of Western Sydney. Thank you to Merlinda Bobis and Nicholas Jose for their generous support. Many thanks to the Australia Council for the Arts. Thank you to the Tyrone Guthrie Centre for peace and quiet. Also thanks to Asialink, Glenfern, Varuna Writers Centre and the Footscray Community Arts Centre where this novella was born. Thank you to Anna Mandoki, Margaret Bearman and Liz Kemp for viewing many drafts. Thank you to Susan Hawthorne, Pauline Hopkins, Renate Klein and the other fabulous women of Spinifex Press. And thank you to Alister Air, my dharma friends and my family for having faith in me.

For more information on Buddhism, Quan Âm and Prajna Monastery in particular, please read *The Novice* by Thích Nhất Hạnh.

*If you would like to know more about Spinifex Press,
write to us for a free catalogue, visit our website or email us
for further information.*

Spinifex Press
PO Box 105
Mission Beach QLD 4852
Australia

www.spinifexpress.com.au
women@spinifexpress.com.au